To
Andrew

Jana Dillon

Upsie Downsie, Are You Asleep?

Upsie Downsie, Are You Asleep?

**Written and illustrated by
Jana Dillon**

PELICAN PUBLISHING COMPANY

Gretna 2002

To Brian, the real Upsie Downsie

*The word "Pelican" and the depiction of a pelican are trademarks
of Pelican Publishing Company, Inc., and are registered
in the U.S. Patent and Trademark Office.*

Library of Congress Cataloging-in-Publication Data

Dillon, Jana.
    Upsie Downsie, are you asleep? / written and illustrated by Jana
Dillon.
        p. cm.
Summary: Mama Mumsie enlists the help of all the other adults in the
neighborhood to help her son Upsie Downsie fall asleep.
        ISBN 1-56554-941-4 (alk. paper)
    [1. Bedtime—Fiction. 2. Pigs—Fiction.] I. Title.
        PZ7.D5795 Up 2002
        [E]—dc21
                                                    2002005319

Printed in Korea

Published by Pelican Publishing Company, Inc.
1000 Burmaster Street, Gretna, Louisiana 70053

It was very late.
"Upsie Downsie, are you asleep?" called Mama Mumsie.

"No," groaned Upsie Downsie loudly. "No, Mumsie, I just can't sleep."

"Still awake?" asked Mumsie. "You poor thing. I'll ask our old neighbor, Miz Crumbsie, to come over. Surely she'll know how to help you fall asleep."

"Oh please, Miz Crumbsie, help my sweet little Upsie Downsie get to sleep."

"Singing a lullaby always works," said Miz Crumbsie in her high, quavering voice. She sat by Upsie Downsie's bed and sang, and sang, and sang some more, until her voice croaked like a frog. Soon, she began to snooze and snore.

"Upsie Downsie, are you asleep?" called Mama Mumsie.

Upsie Downsie was jumping on the bed. He stopped for a minute.

"Noooo," said Upsie Downsie with a loud sigh. "No, Mumsie, I just can't sleep." Then he got back to having fun.

"Oh dear! Our old neighbor Miz Crumbsie has fallen asleep!" said Mumsie. "I know. I'll get the old professor, Mr. Humsie. He'll teach you how to fall asleep."

"Let this be a lesson to you, Upsie Downsie," said Mr. Humsie. "A good-night story always works."

Professor Humsie told many stories. He told about his first teaching job, and his second teaching job, and his third teaching job. On and on he droned, story after story, until he dozed off.

"Upsie Downsie, are you asleep?" called Mama Mumsie.

Upsie Downsie was jumping onto pillows. He stopped.

"Nooo," Upsie Downsie said in a mournful voice. "No, Mumsie, I just can't sleep." Then he started jumping again.

"Oh no!" said Mumsie. "The old professor! He's asleep on the floor! What can we do now? Well, I'll fetch the mayor. He always knows what should be done. He can help you get to sleep."

"Oh please, Mayor Gumsie, come help my poor little Upsie Downsie fall asleep."

"Count!" boomed the mayor. "Upsie Downsie, my boy, count! And then, I promise—yes, on my word as mayor—you, Upsie Downsie—yes, you!—will be asleep!"

So Upsie Downsie and Mayor Gumsie began to count. By the time they reached 207, the mayor's eyes blinked shut for the last time and he began to snore loudly.

"Upsie Downsie, are you asleep?" asked Mama Mumsie.

Upsie Downsie stopped dancing.

"Noooo," moaned Upsie Downsie. "No, Mumsie, I just can't seem to fall asleep." Then he started dancing again.

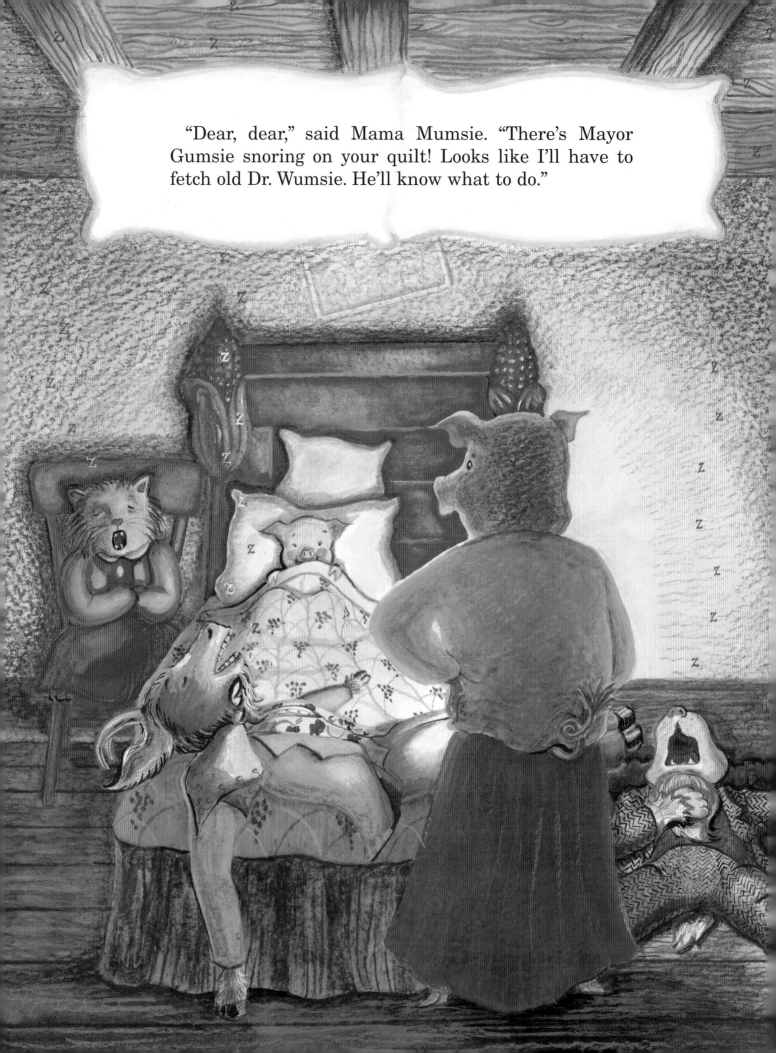

"Dear, dear," said Mama Mumsie. "There's Mayor Gumsie snoring on your quilt! Looks like I'll have to fetch old Dr. Wumsie. He'll know what to do."

"Oh please, Dr. Wumsie, my
dear darling Upsie Downsie simply
cannot fall asleep."

"My prescription is a warm bath," said the old doctor. "It will make you relax, Upsie Downsie. You will feel drowsy. Then you will drift into a deep sleep."

Mama Mumsie dragged out the bathtub and filled it with warm water.

Upsie Downsie soaked in the warm tub. The steam made Dr. Wumsie very relaxed. He felt drowsy. Soon, he drifted into a deep sleep.

"Oh rotten!" said Mumsie, shaking her head. "I will just have to get your father down from the clearing, where he is bowling with the old boys."

Mama Mumsie dragged home Upsie Downsie's papa, Popsie.

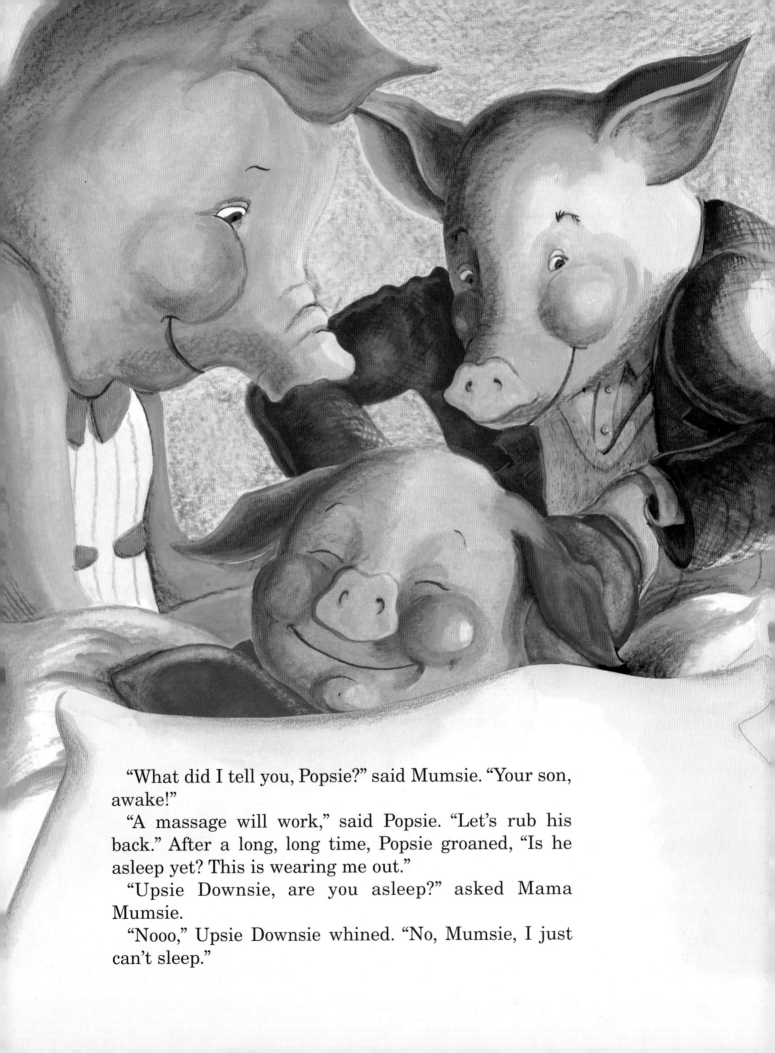

"What did I tell you, Popsie?" said Mumsie. "Your son, awake!"

"A massage will work," said Popsie. "Let's rub his back." After a long, long time, Popsie groaned, "Is he asleep yet? This is wearing me out."

"Upsie Downsie, are you asleep?" asked Mama Mumsie.

"Nooo," Upsie Downsie whined. "No, Mumsie, I just can't sleep."

Mama Mumsie turned to Popsie, but he was lying on the floor, snoring.

"Now what?" cried Mumsie. "I'll just have to go into the forest and bring home the old wise woman, Gypsy Jumsie. She knows everything."

"Oh please, Gypsy Jumsie, my Upsie Downsie can't fall asleep!"

"Listening to the sounds of the night will put you to sleep, Upsie Downsie," said Gypsy Jumsie. "Tell me what you hear."

"I hear the wind whispering in the leaves outside my window," said Upsie Downsie.

"What else do you hear, Upsie Downsie?"

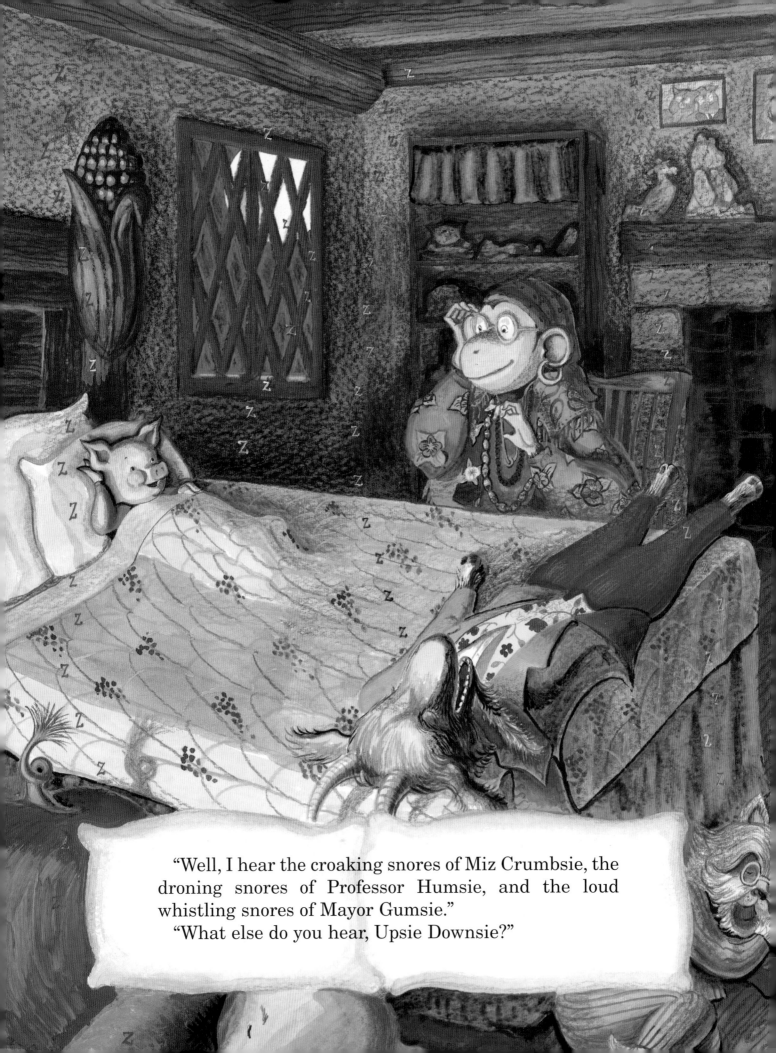

"Well, I hear the croaking snores of Miz Crumbsie, the droning snores of Professor Humsie, and the loud whistling snores of Mayor Gumsie."

"What else do you hear, Upsie Downsie?"

"I hear Dr. Wumsie's sighing snores and the snorting snores of my old papa, Popsie."

"What else do you . . . hear . . . Upsie . . . Upsie . . ."

"I hear the humming snores of you, the old wise woman, Gypsy Jumsie. And . . . I . . . hear . . . zzzzzzzzz."

Mumsie ran to the bed.
"Upsie Downsie, are you asleep?"

Upsie Downsie opened his eyes. "Well, I WAS asleep, Mumsie," he said, "but you woke me."

Mama Mumsie's mouth dropped open.

"But I think I'll close my eyes," said Upsie Downsie, "just for a minute . . . or two . . . or . . . zzzzzzzzzz."

Mumsie pulled the blankets up and kissed Upsie Downsie lightly on the cheek. Then she tiptoed down the stairs, smiling, and made herself a cup of cocoa with an extra-large helping of whipped cream on top.